The Search for Tommy's Shell

By Lin Bailey

New Generation **Publishing**

CHAPTER ONE

As Tommy gazed at himself in his bedroom mirror, he became aware of how scruffy his poor old shell looked, and all the memories of that horrible day came rushing back to him.

It had only been a few weeks ago when it all happened, so it was still so fresh in his mind. A Tear came to his eyes as he recalled how excited he'd been while getting ready to go out with his friends….

"Atichoooo", he sneezed. He still had a bit of his cold left from that awful day….

But a valuable lesson had been learnt - that he should **never** sneeze quite so hard again!

Who'd have thought that just a sneeze could have caused such problems, but it **had** been a **very** big one, after all Tommy was well known amongst his friends as being a bit of a show off (in the nicest way of course). He didn't do anything in a 'small' way.

He was quite a young "leatherback" turtle, so called because of his unusual patterned shell of all different handsome shades of brown.

He was only around two years old, but he thought he was the "Bees knees" (a saying from old fashioned speak-going back a few hundred years or so-which meant someone who was something **really** special-like a prince or something)!

He also had a really good sense of humour, and loved to joke about with his friends, always playing tricks on them. Like the time he asked his octopus friend "Ozzie" if he would kindly get him some shopping as he wasn't feeling too well (deliberately forgetting to give him a shopping bag), which as you can imagine proved to be a nightmare - for his friend Ozzie: He gave him quite a big list - about twelve items, and only enough money to pay for them, but not enough for a bag. Sounds quite a nasty trick to play on your friends but they were all use to him by now. Ozzie should have guessed that he would be up to something.

As you can imagine he had real problems, struggling home - gripping them all tightly with his special suckers, and trying to swim at the same time. What a picture! It took a few weeks before he forgave Tommy for that one.

Ozzie had felt quite embarrassed in front of the all the sea life - poor old octopus! Once he'd got over the embarrassment though, he could see the funny side of it.

Tommy's friends or anyone who had known him long enough knew that they needed to be a bit wary of him when he was at his naughtiest

But despite all his naughty tricks, he was very well loved.

CHAPTER TWO

Returning to his thoughts of that awful day, Tommy remembered how he and his friends: Davina, a beautiful young dolphin whom he had met one day, and fallen madly in love with as soon as he saw her.

She really was beautiful, with shiny skin that glowed in the sunlight beaming down through the water, and her great big eyes that seemed to know exactly what you were thinking before you even spoke, and who swam with grace like a ballerina dancing through the water.

Next, came his friend, Robbie the most handsome, sleek and shiny young ray who was able to glide through the water with huge "wings" like a great bird soaring and turning so gracefully, leaving other fish watching in envy.

His third and oldest friend with him that day, was Martyn the marlin, who had helped him through so many troubles.

He was known as the fastest fish in the ocean, quite large, with handsome silver coloured skin. He could almost fly through the water reaching speeds of up to 100 kilometres an hour, and was about three and a half metres long.

He too was also known to be quite naughty at times because, as he was so fast he would swim up after some of the big fishing boats as they were leaving, with a huge catch of fish in their nets.

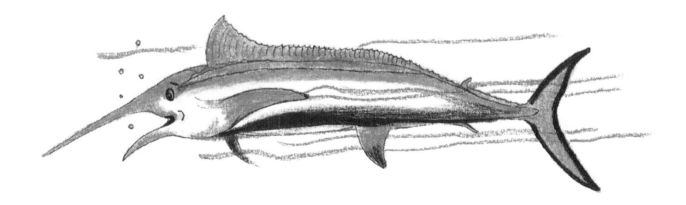

He would grab the end of the net and have himself a nice big dinner from the fish falling through the big hole he'd made in it. What a lazy way of getting his food - clever though, but he was as you can imagine very well respected!

So having introduced you to just some of Tommy's friends, lets get back to the trip they'd all planned the week before.

They had decided that they'd all love to go and visit the coral reef - about an hours swimming time from where they lived, and maybe visit the shopping centre round the other side afterwards - even make a day of it?

It was something they'd talked about for months but just hadn't got round to it, you know what it's like, other more important things crop up.

They had looked forward to it with so much excitement…..

CHAPTER THREE

The big day arrived!

The four friends all got together early for a quick breakfast of crabs legs, and some crabs blood to wash it down with - (well know for giving extra energy) which would help them with their big swim.

Tommy had been feeling slightly tired but otherwise ok.

They all set off together, desperately trying to keep up with Martyn, he did tend to forget that he swam faster than the others!

"Slow down" they shouted, as they struggled to keep up, especially poor Tommy, as he only had short stubby legs.

So, much against his will Martyn had to slow down.

"Anyway this is suppose to be a nice relaxing day out - not a race to see who gets there first!" - Robbie shouted at him.

(He couldn't swim as fast as him if he tried, after all rays swim in beautiful soaring motions up, down and around and swaying as they go, taking time to enjoy the scenery at the same time.)

Tommy was still stood there, in front of the mirror recalling what had happened.

The amazing swim around the coral reef - it had been even better than he'd expected, the colours were …. "out of this world" was the only way he could describe it, like a hundred rainbows all come together in one huge wonderful place.

The sealife they saw were unforgettable; so many different types - and trying to remember them all was hard, there were, some he'd recognised from his favourite film - like a bright orange and white stripey "Clown" fish, and a gorgeous "Blue tang" fish. He also saw a spotted ray who looked just like the one in the film, and …yes! He almost choked with excitement as he remembered seeing quite a large shark too, with scary eyes and huge teeth!

It had felt like he and his friends were actually in the film!

He even spotted other turtles just like himself, although some were a bit bigger than he was, and lots of dolphins like Davina, but none as beautiful as she was of course!

The list went on and on.

But then he suddenly felt a shiver run down his spine, when he thought about what had happened next….

He remembered feeling a bit cold, and his big scaly nose had been a bit blocked up.

The-e-en, all of a sudden he let out the **largest, noisiest**, most ridiculous sneeze that had been recorded in turtle history....

A - a - a - tichooooo- aaaa!! The bit on the end was just for extra effect - he did like to attract attention!

CHAPTER FOUR

Oh dear, oops! ….

There was - all of a sudden, he recalled, a horrible ripping noise and a strange pulling feeling across his back, and as both he and his friends turned to see what was happening, they watched as his lovely shell started to float upwards away from him, as if they were dreaming it.

They stared helplessly as it finally disappeared upwards towards the surface of the ocean.

When the shock finally hit Tommy, his immediate reaction was to throw his stumpy little legs around himself to protect his embarrassment, but as you can imagine that didn't work too well at all. The bits he needed to hide were still in full view as his legs were so short! So to hide his embarrassment, his friends grabbed the largest seaweed leaves they could find and wrapped them around his bare body.

Tommy, remembered turning a nice shade of pink, and was naturally horrified with what had happened.

"You stupid show off!" cried Davina, who was of course just very concerned for him.

"That will teach you **never,** to sneeze so hard ever again!"

He hung his head in shame, as his friends all agreed with her that it really was such a stupid thing to do.

Tommy was, for the first time in his life completely speechless and ashamed of himself.

Davina, Robbie and Martyn felt so sorry for him though…

He looked so desperate, this chubby pink naked turtle wrapped up in seaweed, trying to hold on to some of his pride.

They all helped him swim towards a large clump of rocks where he could rest for a while, and they could all have a chat about how they could possibly, hopefully, try to find Tommy's lost shell.

"Let's keep positive thoughts about this now" said Martyn, the wise and level headed Marlin that he was.

"After all, we need to find poor Tommy's shell somehow; because how on earth he is going to manage without it I don't know."

The other two friends agreed that it would be quite a problem if they didn't.

So they continued their discussion, and it was decided that Martyn would swim up first to see if the shell had hopefully, been washed up somewhere on the shore - then once it was and he'd seen it, he'd report back to Davina and Robbie. They would then continue the rescue mission, and hope like mad that it all went according to plan.

So Martyn left for his swim up to the surface. The other two had stayed behind looking after poor Tommy, who by now had fallen asleep - the awful shock of it all had worn him out.

Once Martyn reached the top he kept his eyes peeled, as he swam as fast as he could to make up for lost time - after all it had been a while since the shell was lost and with the current in the water it could be anywhere by now.

An hour had passed and Martyn had made his way towards one of the nearby islands, he then carried on around it but sadly found nothing.

But as he continued on his search, he suddenly spied something on the surface about 60 feet in front of him….

"Was it"? He asked himself.

He moved forward a bit to get a better view of what he thought was…

"Yes!" he cried out loud, as he realised it did indeed look like a shell - a turtle shell at that, and it just had to be Tommy's, as how many turtles could be stupid enough to lose their shells?!

CHAPTER FIVE

Martyn must have broken the speed limit as he excitedly sped towards the shell. But suddenly, right in front of his eyes a **huge** Pelican - looking like a Pterodactyl (from dinosaur age) as it was so big, dived down in front of him and scooped it up in its enormous beak, as though it only weighed the same as a chicken's egg shell, and just flew off with it.

Martyn screeched to a sudden halt, waves shooting everywhere, and in a dazed state watched helplessly as the thief made off with its unusual catch.

Martyn was in a state of shock for quite some minutes - it's not everyday this sort of thing happens, and once he'd recovered he sadly, slowly made his way back to his friends to let them know what had happened, feeling as though it had all been his fault..

Well, as he expected they were excited to think that he'd possibly found Tommy's shell but completely horrified that a stupid great bird could have made off with it.

Once they recovered they decided that they mustn't give up - at least he'd seen it so they knew it was ok.

They must hatch a careful plan to recover it immediately - before any more harm could come to it.

As Martyn needed a bit of a rest before he went off again, it was decided that Davina would be next to go. She would see if she could find any trace of it, or the dreaded great Pelican who surely would have needed a break, she thought - before taking it much further, as it was a pretty heavy shell. This would hopefully give her a chance to catch up.

So, off set Davina on the same trail as Martyn had swum, her eyes peeled for any sighting of large birds or Turtle shells. She swam as fast as her sleek dolphin fins would take her, towards the area it had last been seen.

Right then, she wished she had a blue flashing light to put on her head - at least it would have moved all the other fish out of the way!

Pausing for air very briefly, she then proceeded to make her way quickly towards the surface, her eyes searching around for anything suspicious. She felt like a detective.

She noticed to her left was an island which she remembered now, from one of her previous swims about a year ago.

Apparently it was known as Palm Island due to the large amount of Palm trees that grew on it. Quite a lot of birds often gathered there to shade under the trees - something drew her towards it to have a closer look....

She gradually swam as close as she could to the shoreline, watching the birds - their wings opened out, to dry the feathers in the warmth of the sunshine.

Suddenly as she swam around the corner she caught sight of one that appeared much larger than the others, it was set back a bit more in the shade of the palm trees.

Davina swam quietly nearer, as near as she dared so as not to disturb it.....

CHAPTER SIX

Whooooah! ….She almost yelled out but managed to muffle her voice at the surprise and shock, as she realised it had to be the huge great ugly Pelican… the biggest she'd had ever seen in her lifetime anyway!

She just couldn't believe her own eyes, at the sight of this great fat thing lying back there sunbathing, with its beak hanging down - the size of a basket ball net!

But it was even worse…

"Huuuh'! Thought Davina, not only was it shading itself from the sun underneath Tommy's precious turtle shell, but there were stinking dead fish around its feet - obviously from its catch much earlier, meant for its dinner. The smell was disgusting. "Yuk"!

"Of all the cheek, of all the nerve"! She kept repeating to herself as she swam back.

"Uuurgh", Davina kept repeating again and again to herself, as she began her fast swim back to report what she had seen to her friends.

They needed to get help quickly, before the sun went down and the thief had a chance to escape with the shell again.

Once back at the bottom of the ocean, Davina broke the awful news to them.

"It had managed to make holes in each side of the shell and had found a way of tying it up between two palm trees, so that it hung across between them"….

Davina continued to tell them

Understandably Tommy was in tears - as you can imagine, at the thought of someone harming his beloved shell - he feared the worst.

So Robbie kindly made him a nice cup of tea, and explained what they were going to do…..

They decided between them that they needed more expert help, and very quickly.

Davina and Robbie would swim back up to keep an eye on the situation, whilst Martyn, being the fastest would go as fast as he could to Tommy's old friend - Todd at his hideaway, not that far from where they were, to get him to help them.

They had already contacted him via a conch shell (the well known way to contact friends and family in the ocean,) and he was only too pleased to help.

Martyn suggested this for quickness - as it was an urgent situation, he could tow him behind by a very strong rope of seaweed, and off he went grabbing at the longer weed as he swam, and in no time at all he had Todd strapped up and ready to go.

(The weed was plaited for extra strength, Martyn was well known for brilliant ideas).

He then wrapped it around his own body and set off, towing Todd behind him on their mission to get Tommy's shell back.

The others, having gone on ahead, agreed to wait till they arrived before doing anything.

Martyn had devised a foolproof plan (he hoped) to rescue the shell and catch the culprit at the same time, whilst everyone else kept a look out, then help out if necessary.

Needless to ask if Todd enjoyed himself - it was the ride of his life!

It's not every day you get strapped up to a Marlin and dragged through the ocean at such a ridiculous speed, he had a permanent grin on his face for days after!

It attracted quite an audience too.

As they zoomed through the water Martyn made up a poem that he started to sing as they swam nearer the culprit:

"We're on our way to save the day,

We'll show you who's boss - we don't give a toss

So give us the shell, or we'll make your life hell

And turn you into a pile of moss"!!

….Martyn thought it sounded scary anyway, and it kept their spirits up!

Todd's family even offered to join in on the mission as back up!

CHAPTER SEVEN

They arrived in front of Palm island and joined their friends, on watch about fifty yards from the shore.

Sure enough, the pterodactyl like creature was still there shading himself with Tommy's shell, and having eaten all its catch of fish, had fallen asleep again with a pile of Fish bones around its feet - what a lovely site!

"So, how do you plan to get the shell back then Martyn" asked Robbie and Davina, dying to know how he was going to do it.

"Not so loud or he'll hear you - I am hoping that if we can get Todd here to crawl up onto the beach, just like turtles do sometimes, he won't suspect anything, " replied Martyn.

"Hopefully, he can creep up and untie the shell, and then once he has, the plan is for him to drag it back to the water - once near the water Davina can grab it too and then we all join in and hang on for dear life"!

"Mmmm" all three of them mumbled - as though not too sure whether it was going to work.

"Well I don't see you all coming up with any better ideas, so we just have to go for it"! Said Martyn as he untied Todd from the seaweed.

Todd seemed to think it sounded like quite a good idea, so they decided to go ahead.

"Go on, go for it and just remember to dig your heels in when you've got the shell, it'll give you more strength and speed to get back down to the water"!

With that he pushed him towards the shore before Todd could think twice about it.

Tod used his stubby but strong legs to dig into the sand, and as he got to the waters edge, just like Martyn had told him.

The sun would be going down soon so he needed to get a move on he thought, as he moved toward the beach - checking first to see what the huge bird was up to.

It was ok; the ugly thing was fast asleep under Tommy's shell.

Even if it did wake and see him, hopefully it wouldn't think too much of it, although turtles are more known to do this at night though….

"Mmmm, Oh well" he thought, he will have to be a little earlier than most - he liked to be different anyway.

So he continued quietly dragging himself up the sand, pausing for a moment, just to check he was still asleep….

Yep, all ok so far, so he grew nearer to the palm tree to the left, pretending he was looking for food, he went behind it and quietly reached up towards the tie holding the shell up on the trunk. He managed to chew most of the way through the tie on that side, until he got round to the other one.

Suddenly he **really** wished he wasn't alone! It wasn't easy, and to think his friends were watching him from the water when he could have done with their help. He felt like some sort of gymnast trying to climb up and around the sleeping beast!

But then he realised that was the easy bit!

CHAPTER EIGHT

He managed to squeeze round to the other tree trunk, holding his breath as he did, he couldn't believe he'd done it without disturbing the "Ugly Beak"- as he had nicknamed it.

He even managed to bite this side of the tie holding the shell, but ….

Oh - oh!! He suddenly realised that he hadn't thought this bit through properly!

The shell slid down slowly, and quietly and landed on "Ugly Beak's" head!

But he still didn't wake - now Todd was in a bit of a panic, and really needed someone to give him some assistance.

Help!! He mouthed to his friends watching him helplessly from the sea.

Why, oh why did he agree to do this, he thought. It was no use expecting them to help they were sea creatures that unlike him could not breathe air for too long, so wouldn't be able to come up onto the beach.

Suddenly - just as he thought it was all going horribly wrong, two huge birds known as "Frigates" had been circling up above and noticed that something strange was going on.

They flew down for a closer look, saw it was a Pelican (who they dislike a lot - as they battle with them over food) and swooped down to the rescue!

Todd was over the moon - was he glad they had appeared; he really thought he was going to be Pelican bait!

Quickly they too grabbed the shell and carefully and quietly lifted it over "Ugly Beak's" head and onto the sand ...."Brilliant"! thought Todd.

Just as they did the Pelican woke up from its deep sleep to see them making off with his new sunshade.

As it struggled, in a sleepy daze onto its huge feet, the three of them managed to drag the shell between them down the rest of the beach and back into the water, where only a few yards further waited Todd's friends - **so** glad to have him back…"Phew - that was so lucky they cried"!

They all grabbed at the shell….bid farewell and a huge thank you to the two Frigates, and disappeared below the surface to return the slightly battered shell to its proper owner, who you can imagine was over the moon.

Well Tommy remembered clearly, the feeling of complete happiness when he saw them swimming back towards him with it, he thought it was lost for ever - It was like all his birthdays come at once….

As he looked it over in the mirror again, he realised how lucky he was to have it back, almost all in one piece, apart from some dents and scratches.

He recalled how he was taken somewhere where it was fixed back on for him - **how** he couldn't remember, but it was back on his little fleshy body - that's all he cared about and his three amazing friends of course!

Lightning Source UK Ltd.
Milton Keynes UK
UKOW06f0158290414

230766UK00008B/46/P